T0143162

KILLER OF DREAMS

A short novel

L O U I S   C I S N E R O S

Order this book online at www.trafford.com
or email orders@trafford.com

Most Trafford titles are also available at major online book retailers.

Good mornin' Vietnam'

Printed in the United States of America.

ISBN: 978-1-4269-4828-2 (sc)
ISBN: 978-1-4269-4829-9 (e)

Trafford rev. 12/03/2010

 www.trafford.com

North America & International
toll-free: 1 888 232 4444 (USA & Canada)
phone: 250 383 6864 ♦ fax: 812 355 4082

To my son Stephen Louis, whom I love

Dad

CONTENTS

ACKNOWLEDGMENT

"How far you go in life depends on your being
tender with the young, compassionate with the aged;
sympathetic with the striving and tolerant of both weak
and strong, because someday in life you will have been
all these."

George Washington Carver

CHAPTER 1

School

The alarm clock went off and the music began, but I felt like rolling over and forgetting about teaching today. The weekend had been a total failure. It went by just like it was a few hours ago. My mouth felt like the 101st Airborne had marched over it and forgotten their officers' latrines. I jumped up and made it to the john where a foul smell of last night's worshipping of the toilet hit me like a howitzer. It turned my gut once more.

I knew I was running late. It was 7:30 a.m. The shower, as usual, was awakening, but the shave irritable. I glanced at the mirror of the man who stood before it-a fucking wreck. My eyes had huge bags that could be used by Oscar De La Hoyas as speed bags. It wouldn't have made any difference to my face. I was getting old. I looked old and tired.

It was a nice autumn day in Galveston. Beachcombers walked along the seashore looking for seashells, the cold waves shuddering on their feet. The ocean's thunderous rhythm on the rocks sent water in the air, making millions of rainbows, as the surfers perched on jetty waiting for the tide to come in, to begin a series of wipe-outs.

Bewitched by the spectacular view, the ocean seized my mind and I began to imagine the savage love affair I could have on the wet sand. The sunrise to my right, and the misty breeze to my left collided on my face and stopped me from fantasizing. I must concentrate on school and not on that wicked woman. Did I have a lesson plan or was I going to brainstorm? Not fully recovered from my fantasy, I felt the agony of my groin ache. The school building was just around the curve. I made it just in time, classes had not resumed.

As I walked toward the classroom, I felt like going back to my car and driving far away. The walls of the school had been defaced over the weekend with graffiti with gang signs

Fucking gangsters!!! I managed to make through the crowd of students to my classroom. I had to get organized before the Animals came in. My mouth still had that sour taste, not to mention the headache that I had. The bell rang before I had a chance to sit down. Holy shit! Here they come.

Minutes later:

"Please students settle down and take a seat and
get ready for the Pledge of Allegiance."
I pledge allegiance to the flag
Of the United States of America and to the
Republic for which it stands, one
Nation, under God, indivisible, with
Liberty and justice for all.

"Class please be seated and turn in your homework so we can begin this morning. We will review the questions you had over the weekend. Also, pass your work to the front."

The students, as usual, began to go through their books making all kinds of racket with the papers. "Class can't you be a little less noisy? Please! Ok, let's get the show rolling. Remember class, that the first question has two parts to it. Also, there isn't a right or wrong answer to the questions, because it's philosophical. So, any volunteers? Patrick, how about you."

Patrick Sullivan was a very good-looking boy with long brown hair that matched his eyes. He had just about every girl on the campus creaming to go out with him. He had been chosen most popular by the student body for the past three years. He also made the varsity squad in his sophomore year and became the star quarterback for the school. This boy had the teachers in the palm of his hand. All he had to do was to flex his muscles and flutter his brown eyes. Except for me. I didn't put up with his shit. **Big Dumb Ass**!

"Patrick, the class is still waiting," I said.

"I don't know, Mr. Gonzales," he answered.

"Why don't you know Patrick? May I ask, did you do your homework?"

"No sir I had football practice."

I was raging. " What does football have to do with the problems in Chechnya? Patrick, you know we studied all last week about the situation in that country. Is it that you don't care, or is football more important?"

"I was tired from football practice, Mr. Gonzales," he answered. The class went into a rampageous laughter with Patrick's dumb answer.

"Okay class, who can help Patrick with this difficult question?" By this time the class was in complete hysteria.

"Kimberly, what did you call the Chechnya's?"

She responded, " Muslim Baby killers; well, that's what my father calls them. My father said that they go around throwing grenades at the Russian service men when they are eating in some of the cafes."

"Kimberly, don't you think that Russian boys throw grenades at them, too?"

"But that's different," she responded naively.

"Kimberly, there's no difference, there're just as dead," I said to her.

'Class since there are many misconceptions about the war, I will reserve the library all this week so you can read the newspaper or check out books on Eastern Europe. Also, I want everyone to make a three-page report on the Chechnya's. It can be on people such as President Bush and Vladimir Putin and their relationships with the war. And its due Friday! That means you too, Patrick!" The students are making faces, those ugly faces like the ones on the dead soldiers. "Before I dismiss the class, I need to talk to you, Patrick. Class, here's your homework on the blackboard. So get to it. Patrick would you please step up to my desk?"

"What do you want to talk to me about, Mr. Gonzales?" Patrick asked?

"It's about you not doing your homework. Also, it's your grades, Patrick. You seem tired and troubled and

I'm concerned about it. Is the practice too much for you, or what?"

"No, Mr. Gonzales," he said very politely.

"Patrick, I had a conference with Coach Peterson about your grades to see if we can't do something about football practice."

'But Mr. Gonzales! We're having our district game this week."

"Yes, Patrick, and you have homework this week, so please do it, so we can win district. Ok?" The bell rang. " Class, you're dismiss . . ."

After an ordeal like that with Patrick, any teacher might pray for early retirement. But without students like Patrick, the teaching profession wouldn't be so rewarding. So, another day, another headache.   In spite of the problems. But drugs . . . that boy is on them, sure as hell . . . I made my way toward the faculty room where I met Coach Peterson. "Coach Peterson, I'd like a word with you."

"Shoot."

Coach Peterson stood six foot five and two hundred and fifty pounds of Texas beef. A former All Americans from Stanford, he never made the pros. There were rumors that he had taken some money or made some side bets on some of the games.

"It's about Patrick Sullivan,' I said as I stood like an ant next to this giant.

What about Patrick?" he asked and turned away from me. It was the beer smell that I still had in my mouth.

"It's his grades. He is not doing very well because of football practice."

He responded." So what do you want me to do? Tutor him."

No coach, just have a talk with him. So he can graduate.

Coach, he needs the credit to finish high school."

"So, give it to him."

"You know I can't do that!"

"Well, what the hell do you want me to do with him?" he screamed at me.

"Coach, just have a talk with him. That's all I'm asking."

"Look bean-brain, that's not part of my job. I'm a football coach. Not a damn counselor!"

Out of frustration I shouted back," Look asshole, Patrick will have to do his work, even if I have to keep him from the game!"

"What the hell is wrong with you? We need him to quarterback. Without Patrick, there isn't a chance to win the district game."

"Tough shit!"

"You sorry bastard!" he shouted and walked off.

Minutes later I ran across Mr. Erickson as I was entering my classroom. Mr. Erickson was the school's Principal and had been for the past five years. Before becoming Principal, he taught social studies and was a damn good teacher. But now, he its on his big fat ass and talks to the superintendent about trivialities. What a waste of talent.

"What's this I hear about you keeping Patrick from the game?" he asked.

"I see you met with Coach Peterson this morning."

"Yes I did and he was pretty upset about it. And I don't blame him. What the hell is wrong with you, John? Can't you and Coach Peterson stop fighting each other and come to a mutual agreement. Why it's a Mexican standoff. John, come to your senses."

"I don't like the man. He's an egoistical asshole. That's all."

"That's all! The man is an All-American from Stanford University, John. Give him some credit."

The question in hand is about Patrick's grade and not Coach Peterson's past or future."

He said with a smile, "That's funny, I received some good reports on him just this morning from his teachers."

Holding back my temper, I shouted back, "That's because they're afraid of him; he's an asshole!"

"Aren't you stretching it out a bit, John? He said with that stupid smile on his face.

"Hell no! Why was he kicked out of Ball High School?" I asked.

"He was discharged because of technicality."

"Technicality! Horseshit! He was fired because he was screwing a cheerleader in the boy's locker room," I screamed at this senile fool. Mr. Erickson's face was turning super red, like an old chameleon who was camouflaging his big nose from a predator. He was still insisting that this jock was a good model for the students and not accepting my opinion that he was a menace to the school.

"And furthermore, we're winning more games than we ever have before," he said.

I angrily replied, "Yes, we're winning more games, but how are we winning them? By giving the football team drugs. The whole damn school knows about what is going on. Open your damn eyes, Mr. Erickson."

Mr. Erickson's face was ready to burst open when he heard what I had said. I could imagine what was going through his mind. Was it true?

"And before I forget, John, there will be a special faculty meeting this afternoon about your allegation. Also, John, please think about your future. You know that Mr. Allen is retiring this year and the position is open for a person of your . . ."

As I walked down the empty hallways of the school I thought I could hear the echoes of the students, but it was only the janitor sweeping the debris from the corners. The ancient man moved very slowly, like if he knew every corner of the building. With a faceless expression, he moved the broom with grace and style that would put any housewife to shame. "Goodnight old man; I see business is picking up," I said with a depressing smile on my face. I knew I had to face the faculty. As usual, the old man just continues to sweep the hall without saying a word.

I entered the faculty room. I smelled the smoldering cigarettes, stale coffee and the horrifying laughter of Coach Peterson. "Glad you make it, John." The room was very quiet. It suddenly dawned on me that this would be a kangaroo court, and that I would be its victim. These damn faceless people.

"Ok people, let's get this meeting over so we can go home. There have been some complaints and allegations by one of our staff. So let's do it."

CHAPTER 2

Drinking Time

After the faculty meeting, I needed a drink or two to calm my nerves. Those damn hypocrites, they know that asshole is giving the player drugs. The evening had fallen rapidly. The heavy fog began to drift toward the inland. The cool ocean breeze whirled around the alleys between the apartment complex in small tornados. A funny thing came to mind. The old man at school. The whirlwinds reminded me of him. Poor bastard. His work is never done.

I'll fix me a scotch and water, turn the tube on and watch the 6 o'clock news. This second hand TV. takes five minutes to warm up. That's good. It gives me time to fix a second drink.

Peter Jennings was giving brilliant commentary on the Chechnya's. As, usual the Russians were getting their asses kicked, someplace called Serzhen-Qurt. The men from the 7th Division had sustained severe casualties in the brutal battle that had lasted for three days. My God! What the hell is President Putin doing. Either

10

finish the damn war or bring their boys back. Damn, this news is **FRUSTRATING**; I guess I'll take a drive to Sam's. Sam's Lounge was where the teachers went to unwind.

As soon as I entered the lounged, psychedelic lights came on from a small lighthouse hanging from the middle of the ceiling. These work electronically when one walks in the doorway.

I started toward the bar. The different colors for the lighthouse were moving counter-clockwise; and this made the Spanish galleons on the wall seem like they were moving toward the bar, where there was a captain's bell that you rang for service. Sam came over to take my order. Sam, the owner of the lounge, was a retired naval captain. He was a huge man with broad shoulders and a beard that made him look like a bear. Sam was a gentle man for his size, and he was as strong as an ox. "Scotch and water?" Sam asked.

"Right."

"How was school?" he asked.

"As usual, no penetration."

A smile came over Sam's bearded face and he said, "Hang in there."

I picked up my drink and walked toward the patio, my usual spot. Here I could stare at the darkness of the ocean and daydream. After a few seconds, a feeling of tranquility came over me as the cold breeze caressed my face. I began to daydream about the women I was making love to on the beach this morning. Just as I was in conquest of this beautiful creature, I felt someone tapping me on the shoulder. It was Sam. I answered with disgust. "Yes."

"Someone brought you a drink," he replied.

"Oh! Who was so kind?"

"Coach Peterson."

"Shit, are you sure it's a drink; or is it quinine, Sam?"

A smile came over Sam's big fat face, as he turned and walked away, nodding his head to reassure me that it wasn't poison. I could see Coach Peterson walking toward me. He had a huge smile on his face and said "Hi, asshole!"

"What do you want?" I said nervously.

He answered with a malicious tone in his voice. "I want you to stop spreading that rumor about me and those damn drugs."

"Those aren't fucking rumors! It's true and you know it."

"Look son of a bitch, you can get me in serious trouble!" he shouted.

"I like your vernacular, Coach. Is that what they taught you at Stanford?"

Like a flash of lighting **WHAM**! The bastard hit me. Oh my God. What was happening to me. I stumbled on to the floor of the patio. The table went crashing to the floor the bottles knocking against the wall. I managed to jump up and pick up a chair and **SMACK**! I hit Coach Peterson on the side of the head with it. He screamed out. "You son of a bitch!"

By this time I was wheezing and gasping for air. Again I raised the chair that I had broken on Coach Peterson' head. **WHAM**! I was hit with a left hook that sent me flying on top of another table, sending glasses filled with bourbon and coke all over me. He was kicking the shit out of me. His foot felt like a Mack truck when it hit me. The pain was unbelievable. I was coughing and spitting blood. Women were screaming and falling on their asses. Coach Peterson was having a field day on my ribs. I managed to pull myself up, trying not to vomit. I staggered down the bar and the half drunk night-clubbers, the parking lot, wondering if I was missing any teeth.

Shit! There goes my dental bill. As I leaned against my car, I heard someone called my name . . . . Holy shit! Another ass kicking. I jumped into my car and started it. Two figures began to run toward the car. I turned the lights on. If I'm going to get an ass kicking, at least I'll know who they are. Dammit! It's Kimberly and Patrick. What the hell are they doing here? They scared the hell out of me!

"Mr. Gonzales are you OK?" Kimberly asked with a frightened tone in her voice?

"Yes." I answered with pain that made my upper lip quiver. Kimberly turned away so not to have to look at my face. Then she said, "Mr. Gonzalez, Coach Peterson wants to hurt you."

"I know Kimberly. He just did a job on my face." Kimberly didn't realize that I was terrified of that maniac. But I kept my composure and said, " Don't worry about me. I can take care of myself."

"Be careful, Mr. Gonzales."

"You bet."

As they walked off, I reached into my shirt pocket for a cigarette. My lip was still hurting, and the smoke burned it. I threw the cigarette out the window. I looked up toward the sky. The moon was surrounded by a circle of fog. The fog had thickened. I decided to go back home like a defeated dog.

I rolled back and forth in my bed, fighting my morning hardness, deciding whether I should call in sick. I could smell the ocean air. I had dreamed about the women on the beach again last night. I heard a light tap on my door and then three more. I managed to get up and put my robe on. Dammit, my lips and ribs ached. I open the door and there stood a tall, skinny policeman with a tablet in hand. "Yes?" I said.

"Good morning. Are you John Gonzales? The owner of the blue Bug license 534 LC? He asked.

"Yes, I am." I answered.

"Sir, I have to inform you that your car has been vandalized," he said with a broad smile.

"What! What the hell you talking about?"

"Sorry, sir."

"But, my car is downstairs."

"Yes, I know. But someone has turned it over completely, sir."

"What!" I screamed at the skinny cop, still not fully recovered from the shock.

"Sir, would you like to go downstairs to see?" the skinny policeman said.

"Yes, goddammit, I would."

The skinny policeman escorted me down the stairs. A thought swept swiftly by my sleepy brain. That fucking Coach Peterson is behind this. My poor Volkswagen was completely turned over. All four wheels were pointed up to the sky-just like the skinny policeman

had said. There was graffiti writing all over the poor "bug." "Damn!" I murmured.

"Sir?' the policeman answered.

"Nothing officer, just thinking out loud."

"Mr. Gonzales, do you have any idea who would do something like this?" the skinny policeman asked.

"No, officer, just help me turn it over on all fours, would you?"

"Sorry Mr. Gonzales, I can't help you but I will call a wrecker for you. Sir, will you sign this report? Thank you."

What an asshole. Doesn't even want to help me. I am a fucking taxpayer. These pigs just go around busting homeless people on the beach. Shit, I'll have to call the school and have someone cover my first period class.

CHAPTER 3

Principal's Office

It took the wrecker seventy-five minutes to get to the apartment and it took him five minutes to flip the car over. He took one hundred and twenty-five dollars from me. What a fucking morning!

Rushing back to school, I began to wonder why someone would pull such a stupid prank.

Could it be some gang members, or was it Coach Peterson? He was big enough to flip it over. I have read articles about teachers having traumatic and psychological attacks by their student and peers. But why me?

I've always been dedicated to my profession. I've always tried to establish a meaningful relationship with my students, to help them strive to develop independence and self-reliance, so they could sustain their interest in education. Shit! Maybe I am just an idealist, or maybe a fool.

I walked up the steps toward the corridor through Smoker's Alley. I felt a certain uneasiness watching the students laughing and running up and down the steps, grabbing each other's asses. The laughter echoed in the hallway, as I entered the Principal's office. I was greeted by Mr. Erickson's secretary, Ms. Cortez. She had a nice personality, very outgoing, but she was very ugly. She had a husky voice, a flat chest and flat ass, and she wore too much makeup. I am not knocking her. She has one good quality she's a good person. That's more than I can say for most people, especially those around this school. There were rumors that she was having a love affair with one of the teachers from the English Department. How kinky! Ms. Johnson handed me a message from Mr. Erickson's desk. He wanted to see me as soon as I came in. Ms. Cortez smiled and winked mischievously at me. There was also a message in my box, a transfer for Patrick to another history class. I was stunned at what they had done to me. It was Coach Peterson who was behind all this shit.

Coach Peterson and Mr. Erickson were smoking as I entered the office. "Have a seat, John," Mr. Erickson said with a smile-that stupid chameleon smile of his. I guess I was his prey and he was going to devour me. I felt uneasiness there with Coach Peterson present. I felt my lips quiver.

"Good morning," I replied, knowing damn well I didn't mean it. As I seated myself next to the doorway, I could feel that they were up to something.

"What ever happened to you John? Did you slip in the shower? Your face looks a mess. You should go see the school nurse."

I could see Mr. Erickson smile. That bastard. He knew good and well that Coach Peterson had beat me up.

"Thank you. I have already taken care of it."

"Oh, by the way, have you read your memo about Patrick's transfer?" Mr. Erickson asked.

"Yes, I did and I don't like it," I replied angrily.

"It was necessary to avoid problems with the boy's parents. You can see that , can't you, John?"

I was ready to erupt like a volcano but I managed to keep cool. I don't know how but I did. The steam was coming out from both of my ears. I was ready to erupt violently, so I got up, threw the memo in the trashcan and walked out. He continued talking to me as I was leaving. He advises me that if I persisted with my accusation about Coach Peterson that there would be disciplinary actions taken by the school board. Also, he advised me to resolve our misunderstanding, saying it wasn't professional to continue such confrontations. He was still bitching when I closed the door behind me. Those unscrupulous bastards!

My ribs and lips were beginning to hurt. I stopped at the restroom to have a look at my disfigured face. The gall of that asshole! He and the school board can kiss my neighbors cat's black ass . . ..Nevertheless, I stubbornly decided to continue my accusation to the school board. My lip was still swollen and I stare in the mirror examining the grotesque mass of flesh.

The day had gone rapidly. As, usual, the students were incredibly uncontrollable, but even more so today. I was in a precarious situation. Students are perceptive animals. They can sense the anxieties and bafflements of a teacher and take and use them for their own benefit. The word had spread like a range fire that I had a fist fight with Coach Peterson and that I had gotten the shit end of the stick . . .. It was in plain view the aftermath of the right cross. I had the class read out of their library books the ones they had checked out, so I wouldn't have to talk too much. Each time I would say something, blood would trickle out. I had use a whole roll of towel tissue on my wound. I could hear the students whispering to each other during class. They were talking about my disfigured lip, and even gave me several nicknames-Blood Alley Lip and, best of all, Monster lip, among others.

CHAPTER 4

Funeral

Last week had been a long one. My so-called peers had alienated themselves from me. It was like I had the black plaque. They didn't talk to me nor eat with me in the cafeteria. They were giving me the silent treatment. I wonder if it would last through the remainder of the school year. God! I hope not . . .

The district game was lost on Friday night–thirty six to fourteen. The team played badly; too many personal fouls, fumbling the ball too many times. Charlie didn't play, he was benched. Patrick had paced up and down the sideline with his head hanging very low. I felt like a heel but nevertheless, it had to be done.

The Friday night dance didn't have the usual spirit. The music was down to earth, Orgy and Creed. I hear Blue Monday about twenty different times. Not even the music picked up the pace. Most of the students were lingering around Smoker's Alley, smoking pot or just bullshitting. My duty was to see that the students didn't get out of hand with their necking at the dance.

I had to talk with some of the members of the school board about drugs on the school grounds. They informed me that there would be a surprise search, on Saturday morning, through the students' lockers. It didn't go too well with the faculty. I didn't mind. Mr. Erickson organized the search. Very much to his surprise, we found a shit load of paraphernalia-ten bags of pot, roach clips made from metal shop water pipes of all sizes and shapes, and even a bag of oregano. All was flushed down the toilet. Several students would be called in to Mr. Erickson's office first thing in the morning on Monday. The search through the lockers was very demeaning to the students' privacy. But it was a precaution. The parents were in favor of having a clean environment for learning.

The Saturday newspaper had a huge article on a former student who was killed in Afghanistan last week. I knew Johnny Miller. He was an average student, very nice and polite. Johnny had given his life to save a patrol that he was on. He had fallen on a grenade to protect his buddies. His body had received all the impact and shrapnel from the grenade. He was given a Silver Star, posthumously, that was send to his mother with a telegram. Johnny's body had come through the Fort Dix Army Terminal during the week. His mother and friends brought his body back. There were rumors that the coffin wouldn't be open because he was missing parts of his body.

The school board decided to let the student body go to the funeral. There would also be a ceremony for his mother in the auditorium. The superintendent would do the honors and dedicate the stadium in Johnny's name for his heroic action in Afghanistan. Johnny's mother would receive an 8" by 6" mahogany plaque with an insignia bearing her boy's name. The plaque would hang in the new stadium's right corridor. The ceremony would be a short one, so the students could go to the funeral.

"After roll call, class, we'll go to the auditorium and I would like you to go in orderly fashion. I want the whole class to sit together. Do you understand? All together!" I said authoritatively. These animals need some discipline. As usual, the students were delighted at not having class. Most weren't even aware of why we were going, just that it was a day off from school. Half the class made their way through the exists of the building toward Smoker's Alley, to have a quick one.

Superintendent McCloud walked up to the podium. Some of the local dignitaries and Councilman Shaw were to present the plaque to Mrs. Miller. The local media was there to cover the ceremony. McCloud cleared his throat to address his young audience.

"On a day like this, when one of our boys dies on the battlefield to stop communist aggression to protect our way of life, I'm proud to call myself an American. I know how Mrs. Miller feels today. She feels proud to have a son like Johnny who died for his country . . .

Pvt. Miller was an outstanding citizen and a good American. He died to protect the freedom, which our young people take for granted. You young people today should be proud; as I am that we have boys like Pvt. Miller in Afghanistan. He should be a model for you to follow."

McCloud paused for a few seconds. His emotions were getting the best of him, or at least

it seemed that way. It was an election year, so the dignitaries gave McCloud a standing ovation. It seemed that he was foaming from the mouth. I had never seen him like that, so melodramatic, so emotional. I knew he was a veteran of the Vietnam War and had had a bad experience there-probably got the clap. But that was a long time ago. The students and staff were shocked at his emotionalism. McCloud resume his speech, but decided to cut it short. "Here to present the award to Mrs. Miller is our distinguished guest, Mayor Johnson."

The students all stood up and gave Superintendent McCloud an enthusiastic standing ovation. Mayor Johnson unveiled the mahogany plaque and presented it to Mrs. Miller. The media went wild with their cameras. The flashes blinded the student body and staff. Mayor Johnson was taking advantage of the media and began politicking for his next election, shaking hands with the staff and with some of his future voters.

Driving with the snake like caravan from Saint James Catholic Church through the small community, toward the cemetery, I still felt nausea from Johnson's emotional eulogy. That disgusting asshole! As the caravan arrived, the honor guard was smartly stationed by the open grave with rifles in hand. Most of the community was there to give Johnny his last farewell. Even the Veterans from Foreign Wars were there.

The priest began his eulogy, blessing the casket. One of the soldiers folded the flag that was over the coffin into a neat triangle and presented it to Mrs. Miller, with a sharp salute. The bugler began to play taps. The shots echoed off the nearby mausoleums. It brought chills down my neck as it rang in my ears. Some of the older people had tears in their eyes. The younger generation stood in the background, laughing and joking around. The burial was short, military one. The crowd began walking away from the new gravesite toward their cars.

Chapter 5

The Devil

I woke up with a scream. God! What a dream! My sheets were soaked with sweat. The horrible nightmare was about Johnny's funeral, but I was the one who was in the casket. I could see that parts of my body were missing. Coach Peterson, Patrick and Kimberly were the pallbearers. I could see vividly that I was trying to get out of the coffin. But Coach Peterson kept closing it. I could see that I was I screaming, blood pouring out of my body. I had pieces of flesh falling from my body. The group was dressed in black robes and their faces were painted red.

Coach Peterson was Lucifer. They were chanting over me, dancing and drinking blood from golden goblets. I could see blood dripping from their mouths. They picked me up from the coffin and placed me in the middle of the pentagram. They began to dance around me chanting. Coach Rodston stood over me with his arms folded on his chest. Kimberly began to dance around me holding a chicken with its head cut off. She then started to rub the blood all over her body.

As the rest started chanting louder and louder, I could see myself trying to crawl from the middle of the pentagram. I was like a worm with its head cut off. All my limbs were missing. Kimberly came toward me; then viciously began stabbing me all over my body. She had an unusual smile on her face. My God, what a dream!

It was like a Stephen King's movie. Still in a pool of sweat, I got up and went to the bathroom to vomit. Taking a long warm shower would help me. Suddenly, a horrible thought came to mind, Anthony Perkins. He would pull the shower curtain and stab me with the knife he used on Janet Leigh. God! I had to get out of the shower again to vomit in the toilet bowl. I manage to empty my stomach of the remaining pizza and beer that I had last night.

Still thinking about the nightmare, the classroom opened as I was correcting the students' homework. It was Coach Peterson, with that diabolist smile on his face. I wanted to smash him in the face. I wanted to pay him back. But a fight would only bring about my dismissal. Made the obvious decision. I got up and faced the blackboard. Coach Peterson moved his bulky body toward me and leaned his weight on me**. WHAM**! He hit me with the back of his mammoth hand. I bounced from the blackboard. I felt the pain all the way to my toes. I found myself on the floor. The pain was unbelievable. Pain on the left side of my face sent flashes to my brain. My face ached. I saw Coach Peterson leaving and I managed to get up and sit in my chair. Tears began to flow down my eyes. What am I going to do about this son of a bitch? My face had puffed up a little. Not very noticeable. But I was horrified. I felt nauseous. The door opened. They came in . . ..

I manage to keep my composure all morning. In the middle of the day I made some eye contact with Mr. Erickson, but he ignore me. I never felt more depressed. I had the idea that I would get an ass kicking every day. But I still had to go on and get that asshole. I was determine to get even. I just had to. My job and my pride were at stake. Somehow I had to persuade the staff and parents about Coach Peterson. I had to fight back . . ..

The empty school corridor was quiet and still. Debris from the candy wrappers was floating in the air. I felt depressed. I didn't even want to leave the school grounds. I was afraid to go to my apartment. It was still early. I had time to drive down the Highway before the fog came in. Suddenly, the door opened and there stood the old janitor with a grin on his face. It was the first time I had seen him with a grin in five years.

"Hi," I said.

He said nothing, just shook the dust from the oily broom and walked back into the building. Some of the students were still leaving the parking lot.

I walked down the corridor toward Smoker's Alley to check if any of the student's was still in the school area. I could still remember last year, when the student's rushed into the Principal's office to demand a smoking area. Their demand was obviously refused. It triggered a protest. The angry students, on their way out of the building, blew out all the toilet bowls from the west wing. They broke windows, and trashcans were set on fire. They assembled in front of the administration building. The police came immediately.

The walkout resulted in the arrest of thirty students on various charges, including inciting to riot, trespassing, vandalism and possession of marijuana. The local police came in paddy wagons and with riot equipment. Several of the students were injured. The walkout lasted for three days. Several of the students were expelled for their subversive activities. Pressure from the community made the school trustees implement the smoking area for these little animals.

CHAPTER 6

Memories

𝕴 lay on my bed trying to forget the whole ordeal that was happening to me. I began to dwell on my childhood to keep my sanity. Could there have been some incident in my childhood that would cause me to become funny? My God! I had a normal childhood. But why am I so attracted to Patrick? Could it be that I am going through latent homosexuality? Or could it be that I admire Patrick for being a super star. He has all the girls that I just dream about. I was born and raised in Refugio, Texas, one of the smallest towns in southeast Texas, population 2050. Historically, it's a Mexican town. Some fifty Texans defended the small Spanish mission from the Mexican dictator, Santa Anna. The result was disastrous for the Texans, as for the missions La Bahia and The Alamo.

My father ran off from his obligations, leaving five fatherless children and an alcoholic wife. What I vividly remember about my father is that he would come in late every Saturday night and beat my mother. He would find her drunk and just like clockwork, he would be arrested for wife beating.

The only thing I really liked about my childhood was running through the woods and swimming in the oily Mission River. My brother and I had a hideout where we spent most of our time bullshitting around. There we spend our time playing Tarzan. We had ropes on every oak tree down the riverbank. There, we would swing and dive into the river like Johnny Weissmuller would after some damsel in distress.

Our African counterparts were three black kids from the neighborhood. Whenever my brothers needed an African uprising, we would invite them. They would paint their faces with white and yellow finger paint. We made African huts out of old corn stalks. After their huts were made, they would capture one of my younger brothers. We would run through the woods. They would follow with their wooden spear. The climax of the uprising would be when I would get on top of the largest oak tree and holler like Tarzan. Then my brothers would stampede the African wildlife, which consisted of a few cows and horses from the nearby pasture.

The woods were full of berries and wild life. Cottontails and Quails were plentiful throughout the woods. My brothers and I would bring down a few of them with our nigger shooters. We were the great white hunters with our primitive weapons.

As the years went by, I grew out of my gawky adolescence. I started working to help support the family at Old Man Martin's Fruit Stand. The fruit stand stood next to Highway 77; Mr. Martin was a crabby old fart, who was half blind in one eye. A fruit crate had fallen on his head some years back. His right eye was damage from the blow. Some of the kids called him one eye jack, because he wore a patch. He was strong for a man in his mid-sixties.

The biggest disappointment in my life was when Uncle Sam decided to draft me into the Army. I spend my tour of duty in Fort Ord, California with the 41st Infantry Battalion. I fell in love with northern California, especially the Monterrey Peninsula and Highway 1. Never had I seen such scenic beauty in my life. I was discharge at Fort Ord and decided to continue my education at Cal Poly San Luis Obispo were I receive a Baccalaureate of Arts in American History.

As the evening fog came inland, so characteristic of Galveston in the fall, the sweet aroma of the hot humid swept by my nostrils, awakening me from my daydreaming. Tears rolled down my cheeks. The salty taste reminded me of Coach Peterson. That asshole! I had to get him fired. I had to convince the school board and faculty. If only I could get one of the players to spill the beans to the school or the police. **Loyalty**! That stupid word. **Loyalty**! They worship him . . .

Chapter 7

Smoking

It was unexpectedly clear, humid morning as I awakened in the middle of my dream. Immediately I jumped up and went to the bathroom to clean up. I felt good this morning. I had made a few calls last night to some of the board members. I had explained my situation with the school and my accusation about Coach Peterson. They ranged from assault to the distribution of dangerous drugs. The members assured me that they would take positive steps to clear the matter up. They would have an inquiry on the allegations. But they said that I had to produce some type of evidence to back my story.

As usual, the biggest festivity was the pep rally in a game against an arch- rival. The anxiety of the students was phenomenal. Their spirits were up. Students were wearing the school colors, football players, and their numbers. Even I felt the electricity flowing through me. I felt proud. Tonight would be up to them to lift the moral following the disastrous defeat of last week. The girls would felicitate their best routines.

I still can remember growing up-football was everything in my hometown. Especially the **Dallas Cowboys** and the hometown team. There were big gambling deals made what team would win; by how many points, and so on. Only the rich Irish would have money to make these types of wagers. My brothers and I would tag along with the boys. We would gather on the dark side of the stadium where we could go under without being detected. Year's back, the gang had made a hole large enough for two to crawl under it. We went in pairs of five minutes intervals. The first pair would signal by whistling that the path was clear. The majority of the time we didn't see the game. The boys started their own game on the side of the stadium. The remarkable thing about it was that we attracted more spectators when the hometown team was loosing. Then the policemen would run us up to the bleachers and confiscate the cup we used as a football.

At the age of sixteen I wasn't very interested in girls. I was still running with the younger boys pulling childish pranks. But once I got an opportunity to meet some girls with this Mexican boy named Manuel. I still can remember the long shower that I took and the after-shave lotion Old Spice that I poured all over my body. I wanted to smell nice for the girls. But my mother had another idea, and she made me take another shower. She said I smelled like a walking French whorehouse.

Manuel was short, skinny boy with a dark pimply face. Manuel and I had made plans at school during lunch. That evening, we made our way to the Mercado to buy some tiparillos. We were going to show the girls that we were **puro macho**. But the outcome of the tiparillos and Old Spice escapade wasn't too impressive. I got damn sick from the small cigar that I never even made it to the restroom. I vomited twelve flights down the bleachers.

Today was a special day for the varsity squad. The squad would be presented with full honors for their athletic ability throughout the year. Some of the members would be receive individual honors for the contribution to the game of football. Others would receive the school's letter. The squad was mostly made up of graduating seniors.

Patrick Sullivan, obviously, would be the first to be introduced. Not that he needed it. It would be the third time he would receive the school letter. Also, he had been nominated for all around Athletic of the Year by the coaches of the school district.

After the brief introduction of the squad, the cheerleaders ran out from the bleachers. They were jumping and tumbling on the track field. There was a short announcement that Kimberly Wilcott would not participate because of an upset stomach. It seemed queer that Kimberly wasn't going to be at the pep rally. She's usually the first to start the ball rolling. I've seen her jump around during a game with a broken leg that she got while skiing in Galveston Bay. And I knew some upset stomach wasn't going to keep her out. There was more to it. I got the feeling that something was wrong. I didn't even see her in the bleachers nor around the stadium. I thought I'd better go down to investigate.

I made my way through the students, as the boys were whistling at the cheerleaders. I didn't blame them. The routine was very arousing.

I ran into Ms. Cortez, standing by the gate. She was there to keep the student's from skipping the pep rally.

"Hi, Mr. Gonzales." Ms. Cortez said with a smile.

The bitch was wearing a see-through blouse, no bra, and tight pants that made her skinny ass look a wee bit bigger.

"Hi, Ms. Cortez, enjoying the pep rally?

"yes, it's marvelous."

"Ms. Cortez, have you seen Kimberly?" I asked.

"Yes, I have. I saw her walking toward the field house a few minutes ago. Why?" she replied very suspiciously. She seemed puzzled by my concern for Kimberly. That overbearing bitch. I can imagine what she was thinking.

Meanwhile the pep rally was at full head of steam, the pom-pom girls were moving their balls of chrysanthemums over their heads and screaming in a ritualistic manner for blood. I made my way through the entrance of the field house, where the odor of sweaty dirty socks crashed against my nostrils. My eyes were becoming dilated from the strong fragrance. Damn, it's funky down here! I see why the players and coaches stay down here for only twenty minutes during the half. Any longer and it would kill you.

I manage to divert my attention from the smell and made my way through the dark hallway. It looked like a medieval dungeon. Coach Peterson's office was small and cozy and surprisingly very neat. There were several pictures on the wall of him when he was in Stanford. Just the presence of the pictures brought chills down my neck. I felt very uncomfortable. My eyes began to scan the room. I notice a book on his desk. It was a library book. It was one that I had recommended last week for a book report on Asia. I picked up the book and found out it had been hollowed out in the middle. How interesting. I began to look around for some evidence. Something that I could pin on him. The first aid kit-maybe there would be something. A syringe or pills . . .. Damn, nothing. Just a bunch of tape and band aids. I better get back to the pep rally.

The hollowed out book was still rambling around in my mind. Why would someone do that to a book? It was a good way to hide drugs or a bag of pills. That's it! That's how Coach Peterson brings his drugs in. I wonder if he sells them to the players. Let's see when the book was checked out. About three months ago. How ironical. There's a war halfway around the world and one right here between Coach Peterson and me.

The afternoon had passed rapidly because of the pep rally. I kept pacing back and forth from my bedroom to the kitchen, wondering what to do. I decided that tonight, during the football game, I would get the police and members of the school board to question Coach Peterson. There they would make an insignificant bureaucratic decision, which would be the dismissal of one lousy coach.

Finally, I manage to sit down and turn on the tube before I wore out the carpet. Suddenly, there was a violent knock on my door. **BANG! BANG!** I jumped to

my feet. What the hell was going on? **BANG! BANG!**
"Who is it!" I screamed.

"It's me, Mr. Gonzales. Patrick! Patrick Sullivan!

I opened the door all pissed off. "What the hell
do you want Patrick, and why aren't you at the stadium?"
Patrick looked pale and sickly. "What's wrong with you?
Come in."

"Mr. Gonzales, Kimberly is dead."

"What!"

"She's dead!"

"Get a hold of yourself, Patrick. Please repeat
what you just told me. But slowly."

"They found Kim dead by the field house after
the pep rally."

"Oh, God, Oh, my God."

Patrick was weeping like some baby who had lost
his mother in some large shopping center.

"Get a hold of yourself. How do you know she's
dead?"

"The ambulance and police are there. I heard
someone say that Kim was dead. They didn't let me near
the place where they found her. It's all my fault that
Kim's dead."

"Shut up Patrick! It's not your fault. Get yourself
together and we'll go to the school."

"No I'm scared."

I felt sorry for Patrick. He was uncontrollable
and he blamed himself for Kimberly's death. If she was
really dead, there would be many questions asked by the
police and I wanted to be there.

CHAPTER 8

Tragedy at School

It was seven-thirty by the time we got to the stadium. Patrick rode silently with his head hanging low. Within ten minutes of our arrival, cars were backed up, bumper to bumper. People had to get out and walked to the main gate because of the massive congestion of autos. Some of the fans didn't know what was going on, nor did I at this time. They were there to watch the football game. Some of the fans started chatting about the last time the two teams got together. It had been a great game. They expected no less this time.

As we made our way through the enthusiastic crowd, a few of the fans recognize Patrick from his pictures in the sports section. The sport columnist had given Patrick praise on his statistic for the year. His passing and touchdown stats were incredible for a high school senior. Patrick was considered the top quarterback in the state. The sports columnist's analysis of Patrick's four years was that he would be the most sought after quarterback in the state by the top rank colleges in the nation.

"Give'em hell Patrick," one fan shouted out as we made our way toward the stadium. We went through the back tunnel to avoid the crowd. The tunnel leads to the track field. There, as we came out into the light, people were running around like they had their heads chopped off. I seized one young girl by the arm and asked her what was happening. But some lady took her by the arm and gave me a nasty look. Some students were being carried out by hand, and others by stretchers. Police were everywhere. My God, it can't be true! My heart began to beat very rapidly. I looked at Patrick. He was white as a sheet. His eyes were red. He had aged about ten years. I notice that the cheerleaders were encircled by the police near the corner of the field house. Coach Peterson and Ms. Cortez were there too. Bewilderment showed in there eyes. I felt sick. A policeman approached me and gave me a soft shove with his nightstick.

"Sorry sir, you'll have to move back."

"I'm a teacher here."

He looked toward Coach Peterson for approval. He nodded. I rushed toward Ms. Cortez. She stood there sobbing.

"What the hell is happening here?"

Still sobbing, she said, "they found Kimberly's body by the field house-nude."

"Was she raped?"

"I don't know John. All I do know is that they took her to the hospital to pump her stomach out. They said she took some pills. They found her purse on the grass near the field house. It had a container with barbiturates."

I looked up at Coach Peterson. "That bastard did it!" I leaped at Coach Peterson, bringing up my right hand and catching him with a quick uppercut. The blow glanced off the side if his throat. Coach Peterson stood motionless for a few seconds, not really feeling pain. I wanted to inflict more pain to his body but within seconds the skinny policeman grappled me down the ground. His skinny arms tightened on the back of my neck. As I screamed at Coach Peterson, "You son of a bitch, you killed her!" the policeman's arm tighten more around my neck

"I will let you up if you behave Mr. Gonzales," the skinny policeman said.

I was making such a scandalous scene. I was kicking and screaming at Coach Peterson. That ridiculous scene brought more police to the aid of the strangler. The skinny cop kneed me in the back, which sent messages throughout my spinal cord. He twisted my arm back. The pain was sharp and to the point.

"Are you going to behave, sir? If not, I will take you downtown and booked you."

"For what?" I screamed!

"For assault, to start with. Now, get yourself together and I will let you get up, Ok?"

Ms. Cortez looked at me with contentment and said,

"How can you accuse Coach Peterson of this."?

"Oh shut up! You were so damn busy waiting for your lover . . ."

"Go to hell you bastard!" she screamed at me.

"Knock it off, both of you!"

Coach Peterson force; himself to stay away from me. He spoke from five feet away. "Where's Patrick?"

I looked around, moving my head right to left and still feeling the pain that this bastard inflicted on my back. 'He came with me. He must've gotten frightened."

I shoved the skinny asshole and began to run through the crowd that had assembled around us. Some of the women started screaming as I made my way through the crowd, knocking over some old fat lady. Behind me, I could hear the skinny policeman's footsteps pounding a long-legged gazelle's, making tracks after me. I made it to the tunnel that lead to the parking lot that was packed with police cars. An impulse made me slow down when I ran into a black policeman. He looked at me for a moment-that steady glance that they give one when they are suspicious. Oh God, I hope he doesn't detain me. The gazelle is behind me.

"Hey, what the hell is wrong with you, running through the parking lot? Don't you know you can get hurt?" the young, black policeman said.

"Yes, sir, but the students are having a riot in the stadium."

"Holy shit!"

The young policeman took off toward the tunnel, holding his three fifty seven steady as it bounced up and down on the side of his leg. Boy, what a dumb jerk!

CHAPTER 9

Cruising

I swung out of the parking lot into the Harbor Side Drive, glancing at my rear-view mirror, taking a second look to check if any blue and white was on my tail. My decision was not an easy one, but I needed Patrick to put the finger on Coach Peterson. My immediate concern was to find Patrick before the police did. I made my reconnaissance along the main drag several times, but no luck.

The sky had darkened and the fog had intensified. I began to worry about Patrick. I had to find him tonight; tomorrow will be too late for the both of us. His safety and my career were on the line. I made my way through the busy intersection of Seawall Blvd where the students hung out on the weekends. I checked a few of the hamburger joints, not a trace of Patrick. Where the hell could he have disappeared? There was no point in going to his home, he wouldn't be there. The police would check there first.

The only place I hadn't check was Bolivar Bridge. As I made the illegal turn, I bounced on the Island and I stepped on the accelerator, dodging cars to avoid a collision.

Bolivar Bridge had a long history of fatalities. During the last two years, the suicide rate among teenagers had risen one hundred per cent. Experts theorized that the increase of drug abuse had a lot to do with the phenomenon. I had visited the Bridge a few times and the view was spectacular. The feeling that I got when I was standing at the edge of the bridge was sensational. The beautiful rainbows were created by the sunlight and the mist; the tumbling rush of the waves on the rocks, echoing in the large pylons off the bridge; the scenic beauty left me breathless.

The waves were like Sirens that lured teenagers to their destruction. There was a small monument in memory of the first teenager who had leaped to his death. The boy was from somewhere in the Midwest.

The illumination from the cars blinded me momentarily. Then I notice a lonely figure on the ramp of the highway as I passed under it. I couldn't tell if it was Patrick. It could easily be some damn homeless veteran. But I decided I better make sure. I still had to go a quarter of a mile to the next exit. It took me a few minutes to get to the turnoff. I downshifted into second gear as I whirled around the ramp toward the entrance of the bridge. My Volkswagen began to backfire and smoke began to slow down. Poor devil, it'd taken hell these past years.

Sure as hell, it was Patrick! He recognized me and started walking faster as I drove next to him. He still kept moving. I shouted and opened the door. "Get your ass in, Patrick" Patrick stubbornly continued walking. "Patrick, please get in."

"Why don't you leave me alone!"

"Look, I'm trying to help you."

"Don't give me that shit, Mr. Gonzales!"

"C'mon, get in and we'll go back to my apartment and we'll talk about it." I managed to convince Patrick and we started home.

The fog was so heavy it was like a gigantic tidal wave. Every few feet there would be a clearing and then **WHAM!** A heavy cloud would swallow my Volkswagen. I had never seen the fog this heavy before. I made a u-turn back into town. Patrick glanced back and noticed two small lights that were cutting their way through the fog. The lights were getting much larger at a very rapid pace.

"I think someone is following us, Mr. Gonzales."

I glanced in the rearview mirror. Sure as hell, there was an automobile behind. I took a turnoff on Ocean Drive that lead toward the beach. The lights that were following turned off too. There was an embankment that the surfers used to drive down on the beach. I headed toward it. Unmistakably it was Coach Peterson behind us. I recognize his dune buggy.

I drove up the embankment, a forty-five degree angle, downshifting to second gear to get maximum acceleration. As I downshifted, my left hand stuck on the wheel. I was sweating nervously. I was scared. Damn scared. Patrick's baby brown eyes seemed much larger than usual. He was holding on to the seat like a small chimpanzee.

I don't know how my bug made it to the top of the embankment, it was blowing smoke in all directions, farting and shaking the hell out of us. At one point, it seemed that we weren't moving. The ram needle was jumping back and forth. I flooded the gas pedal to the floorboard. The old bug just lost its stuff. Then, the beach was in front of us. I slam-shifted into the third and kept my foot on the pedal. I never used my brakes, I didn't have to. They were shot. The sand would slow us down. So there was no need to worry. The immediate danger was behind us.

We were going down in an incredible pace. When we got to the base of the embankment, the nose of my bug **CRUNCHED,** leaving the right fender twenty feet behind us. My foot was frozen to the pedal. If the old bug did not let us down and not stall on the sand, I swore to God, I'd give it a transplant.

There was sea drift and seaweed all over the beach. Some of the seaweed managed to entangle itself in the rear wheels. It was flip-flopping every which way, but I didn't let it bother me. I had my hands full zigzagging around the driftwood, smoking a few pieces with the right tire. With an unexpected **KABLOOM,** a huge spray of beach water was sent upwards like a huge wave. My first reaction was to grab the steering wheel tighter and close my eyes. My God! I just run into the ocean! The windshield cleared to reveal that it was just a tidal pool that lead into a large pylon. The old bug stalled out on me. We have to get the hell off the pylon. I could see the dune buggy's light a few hundred yards away. I grabbed Patrick's arm. "Let's get the hell out of here," I shouted!

Patrick jumped and slipped on some slimy green algae and fell on his butt. "C'mon, move," I screamed at him. The water came up to our knees; it was damn cool. I reached back into the car. I opened the glove compartment to get my flashlight. I hoped and prayed my batteries were working. Patrick and I began to move further onto the pylons. They seemed angry. The impact of its force pounded the bridge. The further we move on the bridge, the darker it got. I didn't dare use the flashlight until it was necessary.

"Patrick, come out and I'll help you," Coach Peterson yelled!

The echo sent chills down my back. "Don't you believe that shit, Patrick."

"But Mr. Gonzales, Coach Peterson hasn't done anything."

"My God, Patrick, your girlfriend might be dead because of that lunatic! C'mon, move, he's right behind us." Now I had to use the flashlight. The darkness of the night was too much strain on the eyes. "Look, there's a large crevice; we'll hide in there."

"Mr. Gonzales, why don't you believe me? Coach Peterson hasn't done anything.

"C'mon, let's get in there. He'll never find us. We'll stay until he leaves."

Minutes later, we got as comfortable as we could on the sharp edges of those damn rocks. The rocks were spearing our rumps. But there was no room enough to stretch our legs. The waves were beginning to fade from my mind. My God, what a night! I just couldn't believe that I could be in this unusual position-in some dark crevice, with a wet-nosed kid, the entrance blocked by some lunatic. Things had to get better.

CHAPTER 10

Kiss of Death

I woke up freezing. The wind was blowing fiercely, howling between the pylons. The damn tide was up. The water was splashing against my leg. My God, there was no way out! We were trapped like rats.

"Patrick, move your ass before we drown!" Patrick got a kiss; **SMACK** a wave hit him with tremendous force, sending him onto his back. I grabbed his arm before the swell swept him away.

"Are you Ok, Patrick?"

"Yes, what are we going to do?"

"Well, we're not going to stay here, that's for sure. We're going to swim like hell. That's what we're going to do. So pray like hell, and get ready!"

"We're going to drown!"

"Shut up!"

SMACK! A swell covered us with a tremendous force. I managed to hold onto a hole in the crevice. My hand started slipping as the swell lifted me up. I could feel the anger in the wave as the next one came and slaps me in the face.

KABLOOM! The large swell covered us. I was holding as tight as I could to the rock. "Ok, let's time the wave. Well, take a look at your watch!"

"It's not working!"

"Fuc-kkkk! Let's go." We jumped into the water. It was waist high and very cold. Another wave was coming and it looked much larger and the wave lifted us up. I could feel the undercurrent sweeping me back. I manage to surface my head and get my balance on the base of the pylon.

"Look, Mr. Gonzales there's your Volkswagen!"

The damn thing was floating right in the middle of the pylons. That lifted my spirits.

"Swim to it!" I shouted to Patrick.

The current was taking its toll on my legs. I felt them giving up under it's force.

I manage somehow to get to the old bug. I was holding on to fender, giving Patrick a helping hand, one welcome to a very exhausted boy. The bug was caught on some seaweed that managed to hold it in place. The bug was rocking from side to side, which made it difficult to hold on to. The entrance of the bridge was about fifty feet away. I was too tired to fight.

I manage to get to the door of the bug and opened it. I jumped in to see if I had some dry cloth. No such luck. Not even a pair of dirty socks.

"Mr. Gonzales! Look, what's floating over there? It looks like Coach Peterson!"

My God! I jumped in the water and moved toward the huge body of Coach Peterson. He was floating face down. I knew then that he was dead. I turned his body around. He had a huge cut on his forehead. His eyes were rolled back behind his sockets. He must have slipped on that green algae and hit his head and drowned last night. I tried to move his huge body, but something was holding his legs. They were wrapped around in the seaweed.

"Patrick, come here and help me with Coach Peterson. His legs are stuck in the seaweed." Damn he was heavy, his body had swelled up with the water he had swallowed.

As much as I hated him, I felt like crying. And I felt sadness for Patrick, who I knew worshipped him.

"What are we going to do, Mr. Gonzales?"

"First, we have to get out of here and call the Highway Patrol. Patrick, do you know a way out of here?"

"Just the way we came in. But what are we going to do about Coach Peterson's body?"

"We can't carry him. We'll just leave him here. We'll call the police and tell them what happened. They'll know what to do."

The ocean breeze grew fresher and cleaner as we made our way to the embankment.

"Maybe we can wave a Smokey down, Mr. Gonzales."

"I hope so, Patrick, I'm not young as I would like to be."

"You're doing Ok for an old man."

"Ha Ha Ha."

"What's so funny, Mr. Gonzales?"

"Oh nothing. Just that you have a traveling companion."

"What?"

"There's a starfish stuck to your ass."

The station attendant didn't notice us when we entered the office. He was dancing to some music from LIL Wayne. The rhythm of his head and the snapping of his fingers were in sequence with the music. If you call rap, music. He seemed to be in trance, his head bobbing with the sound of the song. The music was loud and not very soothing to my waterlogged ears. There was such a contrast to the sound of the ocean waves that I could still hear splashing against my eardrums.

The station attendant was a young black kid who had a huge natural and iron comb stuck in it. He seemed to be out of a Lion King movie. "Yeah Dawg! What are you doing here? How come your wet?" he asked.

"We took a midnight swim," Patrick responded.

"You're shitting me dawg! What wrong with you honkies? You're tripping. My boss don't like people who are loaded," responded the black kid as he started combing his hair.

"Yeah right, do you have phone?" Patrick asked.

"Say don't I know you? You're Patrick Sullivan, the quarter back! What happened to the game last night? I hear last night that the game was postponed till next week. I can see why. You were out swimming in the damn ocean. Man, you're fucking up my bet. I got twenty-five on your ass to win by seven. So man, don't fuck me up on my green. The phone is outside by the restroom. Yeah man, you got some weed on you?"

Patrick looked at him and said, "I thought your boss didn't like people that were loaded."

"That's my boss, but not me. I dig that shit. You have any marijuana or ecstasy?"

"No Dawg, I don't touch that stuff," Patrick said.

I pulled out a five-dollar bill from my wet wallet and handed it to the young attendant for some change. I made my way to the phone booth, from where I would have to explain this nightmare to the police. The coffee that Patrick bought was good. It was giving new life to my numb body. Black and strong. I would need strength for the next few hours, not just for myself but also for Patrick. I deposited the thirty-five cents in the slot and dial 911 for the operator. "Operator, this is an emergency. Would you contact the Highway Patrol for me? Thank you."

It didn't take the Highway Patrol and the Galveston Police long to get to the scene. Moments later, the Coroner arrived. They took us to the station of the Galveston police for questioning. After a few hours, they released us pending an inquiry into the death of Kimberly and Coach Peterson.

The morning was beautiful, the sun burning through the fog. I felt like shit, sleepy and tired. I managed to get a yellow cab. The cabbie was a typical Texan. He wore a large Hawaiian shirt and sneakers, and drove like hell. He was rocketing down the street, blasting in and out through the residential neighborhood. The streets were deserted except for a newspaper boy pedaling his bike, trying to escape a Chihuahua, leaving newspapers scattered all over the sidewalk. The Chihuahua would momentarily stop and ravage one, then continue to pursue the biker. Within a few minutes, the cabbie stops in front of my apartment. It was nice to be home.

"Did you hear the news last night? President Bush committed 25,000 troops and invaded Iraq." The cabbie said

"Damn, more boys are going to die," I answered.